ESCAPE FROM PLANET BOGEY

To Cerys and Megan on chocolate worm farm – GPJ

To Andy and Jackie, for encouraging and putting up
with me! – SM

STRIPES PUBLISHING
An imprint of the Little Tiger Group
1 Coda Studios, 189 Munster Road,
London SW6 6AW

A paperback original
First published in Great Britain in 2017

Text copyright © Gareth P. Jones, 2017
Illustrations copyright © Steve May, 2017

ISBN: 978-1-84715-787-4

A CIP catalogue record for this book is available
from the British Library.

Printed and bound in the UK.

10 9 8 7 6 5 4 3 2 1

GARETH P. JONES
ILLUSTRATED BY
STEVE MAY

Stripes

PET DEFENDERS

Protecting those who protect us

Did you know that Earth is under constant alien attack?

Don't worry.

We are the Pet Defenders, a secret society of domestic animals. We are your dogs, cats, rabbits and rodents. While you are off at school or work or doing whatever it is you humans do, we are keeping the Earth safe.

We keep our work hidden because we know what humans are like. The first sight of an unidentified flying dung saucer or an invasion 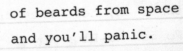 of beards from space and you'll panic.

Before you know it, you'll have blown up the very planet we're trying to defend.

Just carry on as normal — stroke your cats, take your dogs for walks and clean out your hamster cages. Don't forget to feed us, but please … let *us* take care of the aliens.

Now that you know all this, we need you to forget it. Our specially trained seagulls will take care of that. Ah, here they are with the Forget-Me-Plop now…

SSSPLAT!

CHAPTER 1

THE MEAT GRAB

Mitzy waited behind the wall, ready to pounce. Any moment now, the butcher would place the bin bag on the step then go back inside. There would be just a few minutes before he carried it to the big metal bin out the back.

Every scavenger in Nothington-on-Sea had tried and failed to get that bag but Mitzy was no ordinary alley cat. She was a Pet Defenders agent. If she could prevent a gigantic dung beetle from swallowing the Earth and thwart an army of alien beards, she should be able to make the meat grab.

Unfortunately Mitzy was not alone.

"So how are we going to do this, partner?" squeaked a scrawny grey rat.

"Don't call me that," snapped Mitzy.

"I get it. You're a loner just like me," said the rat. "The name's Crisp by the way."

"Well, Crisp, I've already got a partner," said Mitzy. "Now, if you don't mind, I'm pretty hungry and—"

"Where is he, then?"

"Who?"

"Your partner?"

Mitzy sighed. "Biskit has an owner," she replied curtly.

"Biskit? Funny name for a cat."

"He's not a…" Mitzy stopped herself. "What kind of name is Crisp anyway?"

"My family lives under a Chinese restaurant, see. My mother named us after things on the menu. I've got a brother called Chow Mein and a sister called Pork Balls."

"Where are crisps on a Chinese menu?" asked Mitzy.

"My full name is Crisp E Duck." The rat chuckled.

"You're lucky I don't eat rats otherwise you'd be on my menu." Mitzy licked her lips threateningly but Crisp casually brushed his whiskers.

The back door opened and the butcher placed the meat on the step. It was securely tied up in a thick plastic bag but the smell was so strong it made Mitzy's stomach grumble. It took all her willpower to remain hidden but the temptation was too much for Crisp. He edged out.

"Argh. A rat!" yelped the butcher. "Get away, you filthy thing."

Crisp scurried back under the bush while the butcher picked up the bag and carried it to the bin. The lid **CLANKED** shut and the butcher went back inside the shop.

"Nice work, Crisp," muttered Mitzy.

"I'm sorry. I couldn't help myself."

"Maybe I can't help myself." Mitzy extended her claws and took a step towards the rat, letting out a threatening purr.

"I hope I'm not interrupting dinner," said a voice from behind her.

Mitzy turned to see a scruffy brown-haired dog sitting on the wall, his tail flopped over the side. He smiled.

"Biskit," said Mitzy.

"*This* is your partner?" said Crisp. "But he's a dog!"

"He's sharp, your friend," said Biskit, jumping down and wagging his tail cheekily in Crisp's face.

"He's not my friend," replied Mitzy. "He's just a rat whose belly is bigger than his brain."

"Hey, that's not fair," protested Crisp. "Mum

says I'm the smartest member of the family. Well, except for Veg Dumplings."

"Come on," Biskit said, ignoring the scrawny rat. "Commander F wants to see us."

Mitzy turned to leave but Crisp burst out, "Who's Commander F? Hold on, who *are* you two?"

"It's none of your business," said Mitzy.

But at the same time, Biskit replied, "We're Pet Defenders."

"Pet Defenders?" exclaimed Crisp excitedly.

Mitzy threw Biskit a disapproving glance. "We're supposed to be a *secret* organization."

"Wow! I've never met a real life Pet Defenders agent before," said Crisp. "Wait until I tell my half-brother, Chop Suey, about this. Can I have your paw prints?"

Mitzy lowered her head and pushed her nose up against the rat's face so that her whiskers brushed his cheek. "You're not going to tell anyone anything. Got it?"

"S-s-sure," Crisp stammered, his nose twitching nervously as he edged away from Mitzy. "Mum's the word. I won't tell a soul. Your secret is safe with me. Hey, so have you met actual aliens? Like in real life? What was that like?"

"Terrifying," said Mitzy, as Biskit said, "Brilliant."

"Crisp, we do what we do so that you don't

need to know what we know," said Mitzy.

"Eh?"

"Just go and find something to eat," she said. "And forget you ever met us. OK?"

"I'll never forget this," said the rat.

"See you around, Crisp," said Mitzy.

She sprang up on to a wall then dropped down the other side. Biskit followed. "Have you eaten?"

"I'm fine," said Mitzy. "The job comes first. Let's go and find out what Commander F wants."

CHAPTER 2

ONE HUNGRY RABBIT

The Pet Defenders took a secret route across town to the garden where Commander F kept his Hutch Quarters. They walked along walls and ducked down the back alleys and side streets of Nothington-on-Sea. As they passed a kitchen window, delicious smells drifted out and Biskit heard Mitzy's stomach growl. He felt bad for her. He had devoured three bowls of Chum Tum Yums before leaving the flat.

"You know you could probably find a new owner if you put your mind to it," said Biskit.

"No thanks," said Mitzy.

"Oh, come on," said Biskit. "Most of the cats round my way have at least three houses they visit."

"I'm not like that," said Mitzy. "I have an owner. She's just missing."

Biskit nodded and smiled understandingly. He felt the same way about his previous partner. The difference was that Champ had stepped into a portal and been transported across the universe. There was probably a more down-to-earth explanation for the disappearance of Mitzy's elderly human owner, Cynthia.

"I don't like the idea of you fending for yourself out here," said Biskit. "The agency uses pets because pets don't need to worry where their next meal is coming from. We can concentrate on the big alien stuff."

"There's more to being a pet than eating tinned food," said Mitzy. "It's about being loyal to your owner."

"I suppose." Biskit shrugged. "I just don't know that many loyal cats."

"You know one," said Mitzy pointedly.

When they reached HQ, they found Commander F sipping water from a pipette in his hutch. "Agents Biskit and Mitzy," he said, "I don't suppose you brought any food, did you?"

"Sorry," said Mitzy.

"Shame. Emily has got me on this Every Other Day diet and today I'm only allowed water. It's not natural. I've a good mind to report her for animal cruelty."

"You wouldn't do that," said Biskit.

"No, you're right." Commander F's tone softened. "She means well ... but I'm so hungry I could eat a field of radishes." The large white rabbit leaned forwards and whispered, "And I hate radishes."

Biskit backed away. "Fascinating, I'm sure ... but why did you call us here?"

"Oh, just to tell you I don't need you at the moment." Commander F scratched his ear with his foot. "The only report we've had all week was a gerbil who claimed to have seen strange lights in the sky."

"Don't tell me, it was a plane," said Biskit.

"Stars," said Commander F. "No, it's very quiet. You two may as well take some time off."

"You dragged us across town to tell us that?" exclaimed Biskit.

"Ye-ess," said Commander F. "And also because I was hoping you might have some food. I've eaten all of next door's cabbages now. They blame it on their dog, of course."

"Ha, that Alsatian is so thick he probably thinks it *was* him."

"He does," said Commander F with a chuckle. "I've heard him talking to himself about it. *Why did you do it, Larry? Why did you eat the cabbages?*"

Mitzy scowled. "The poor thing must think he's going out of his mind."

"It wouldn't be far to go," said Biskit. "He's so stupid he thinks his tail is following him."

"Yes, I've seen him try to creep up on it," laughed Commander F.

"You two shouldn't be mean to him just because he's not as clever as you," said Mitzy.

Commander F turned to face Mitzy. "It's us being clever that keeps dogs like him safe from alien attack," he snarled. "Now, I suggest you take your time off before I change my mind."

Biskit and Mitzy slipped under the fence and stepped out into the street. Biskit stopped to sniff a lamp post while Mitzy inspected a discarded crisp packet for traces of food.

"What will you do with your time off?" she asked, licking a couple of crisp crumbs.

"Three words," said Biskit. "Park ... stick ... fetch."

"Dogs are so weird," said Mitzy. "You get given time off from chasing aliens and you want to spend it chasing sticks."

"Just go and find something to eat," said Biskit. "You get as grouchy as Commander F when you're hungry."

CHAPTER 3

CRISP'S SNEEZE ABDUCTION

Mitzy was back on the hunt for leftovers. It was never easy — most bins were designed to keep animals out. Mitzy was sniffing around the back of a fish and chip shop when she heard something quietly sobbing. She spotted a small grey animal inside a paper cup.

"Hello?" she said, approaching.

"Wh-wh-who is that?" squeaked a voice. "Wh-wh-what do you want?"

"Crisp? Is that you?" asked Mitzy.

The rat emerged from the cup. "Mitzy! You've got to help me. It came out of nowhere then it… Oh, it's too horrible to say… It *sneezed* on me."

"What sneezed on you?" said Mitzy.

"I don't know what it was." Crisp shuddered.

Mitzy noticed that his fur was damp and he was covered in slime.

"You have to protect me," said Crisp. "This thing … it wasn't –" he lowered his voice and scurried forwards – "it wasn't from this planet."

"Crisp, I know you've had a shock," said Mitzy, in a soothing voice. "But I need you to describe what you saw."

"It was the size of a human and had tentacles instead of fingers, but it was the nose I remember most."

"The nose?" said Mitzy.

"Yes, a huge long nose. I'll never forget it. It sneezed and covered me with goo then … everything went really weird."

"What kind of weird?"

"Like being sucked up and spat out by a rainbow trapped in a tornado." Crisp whimpered at the memory.

"Oh, that kind of weird." Mitzy scratched her ear with her back paw. "What happened after that?"

"I wasn't here any more." Crisp's voice wavered.

"You weren't where any more?"

"I wasn't where I was."

"Where were you if you weren't were you were?" Mitzy asked, feeling more than a little baffled.

"All of a s-s-sudden I was in this place like a huge football stadium f-f-full of big-nosed aliens … and everything was green – even the sky! There were crowds of these aliens sitting around the sides of the stadium, then one of them s-s-spoke."

"What did it say?"

"It asked what kind of animal I was. I said I was a r-r-rat."

"What did it say to that?"

"Nothing! It sighed then made a honking sound and s-s-sneezed on me. When I opened my eyes again, I was back here."

Crisp was so engrossed in his story that when a window opened, he almost jumped out of his skin.

"Crisp," said Mitzy softly. "You've had a scary experience but you're safe now."

"Safe? How can I be safe while that thing is out there?" he said frantically, scurrying round in a circle.

"Because I'm here to protect you. If you do exactly what I say, you'll be fine. OK?"

Crisp nodded vigorously.

"Now wait here. You see the bird up on that roof?" Mitzy nodded at a seagull. "In a minute it's going to drop a substance called Forget-Me-Plop on your head. It will make all this go away."

"My memory's going to be wiped by bird poop?" exclaimed Crisp.

"Crisp," said Mitzy calmly. "You have to trust me. Stay where you are."

Mitzy gave the seagull a signal and watched as it swooped down and dropped its load on Crisp.

"Eurgh," he said. "This day just gets worse and w…" As the Forget-Me-Plop took effect, a blank expression fell over Crisp. "What was I saying? Who are you? What's going on?"

"I was telling you that the bins on the high street have blown over," said Mitzy. "If you hurry, there's plenty of food down there."

"Really? Oh, great. Thanks, er, what was your name?"

"It doesn't matter. See you around, Crisp."

Ignoring how hungry she felt, Mitzy made her way across town to the block of flats where Biskit lived with his owner, Philip. She climbed a tree that overlooked the flat. She could see Biskit and Philip getting ready to leave. Biskit was all jumpy and excitable at the prospect of spending the day with his owner. Mitzy remembered that feeling. She never went for walks with Cynthia but she used to love curling up on her owner's lap and listening to her sharing her innermost thoughts. When Cynthia talked of her fears about being put in a retirement home, Mitzy comforted her with a reassuring purr. Mitzy missed that.

They stepped out of the door and Philip bent down to ruffle Biskit's fur. "Who's a good boy?"

"Me," barked Biskit. "I'm a good boy."

Mitzy stifled a giggle. Pets always behaved

differently with their owners than with each other but it was still funny to see Biskit with such a big dappy grin. She didn't have the heart to drag him away from his day with Philip.

"What do you say, boy? Park?"

Biskit was happy and Mitzy wasn't going to get in the way of that. She would investigate on her own.

CHAPTER 4

BISKIT'S DAY OFF

Philip had picked a good stick. It was just the right size to get a long throw. Not too bendy. Not too leafy. The whistling sound it made as it soared through the air was like music to Biskit's ears. He chased after it then leaped up and grabbed it between his teeth before coming down again, twisting around and bounding back to Philip to repeat the whole thing. It was wonderful.

"It's going to be a really big throw this time," said Philip. "You'd better be ready."

Philip threw the stick, sending Biskit charging

straight through a football game, over a bench and into a small patch of woods. He lost sight of the stick but he wasn't worried. He could sniff it out. Biskit picked up Philip's scent and began to follow it, but when he looked up he saw another dog had the stick in his mouth.

Biskit stopped in his tracks and stared at the puppy, who dropped the stick.

"Stick," yapped the puppy. "I like sticks. I like this stick. You want to play with my stick?" Seeing the expression on Biskit's face, he paused then said, "Oh, sorry, is it your stick?"

Biskit kept staring. He was an Old English sheepdog, except he was a pup, so actually he was a *young* Old English sheepdog. He was all bouncy, panty and tail-waggily. But it was the pup's eyes that reminded Biskit of his old partner. Biskit remembered the last time he had seen Champ. They had been investigating a fox's report of unusual behaviour in the park. Biskit hadn't believed him – foxes were unreliable witnesses at the best of times. But Champ had wanted to do things properly and investigate the situation.

They had split up to take a look around when Biskit had seen a flash of light around the side of a café. As he rounded the corner he had seen Champ vanishing into a circle of swirling colours. He had called out to him but the portal had closed and Biskit had been left staring at a wall.

"Er, I'm sorry about picking up your stick,"

said the puppy, wagging his tail. "But … why are you staring like that?"

"I'm sorry," said Biskit. "It's just that you remind me of someone I knew… I know."

"Oh, I see. Chomp," said the pup.

"No, Champ. Wait a minute. What?"

"My name is Chomp."

"Chomp?" repeated Biskit.

"CHOMP!" A child was calling.

"That's my owner. I'd better go. Nice to meet you! Sorry again about your stick."

He turned and ran into the arms of a little boy who Biskit recognized at once. It was Champ's owner. And then it dawned on Biskit – Champ's family had replaced him. They didn't know about the alien stuff. They just thought their dog had run off so they'd gone out and bought another one. Champ had been replaced as though he was a broken-down car or a faulty television.

"BISKIT? There you are! Was that one too far for you?"

Biskit picked up the stick and dropped it at Philip's feet. Philip bent down but instead of picking up the stick, he patted Biskit's head and ruffled the hair under his chin.

"I'm glad we've had this day together," said Philip, "because I've been meaning to tell you, I've booked a week's holiday. It's a last-minute thing."

"A holiday?" Biskit barked. He felt excited at the idea. Commander F wouldn't be happy but what could he do?

"Anyway, I'm flying," continued Philip, "so I can't take you but I've found a great little kennel."

Biskit took a step back.

"It's a really nice place," said Philip.

Biskit let out a sharp bark. "A kennel?"

"It'll be a holiday for you, too."

Biskit growled, then he turned and ran.

"Biskit!" Philip called. "Come back. I'm sorry!"

But Biskit didn't stop.

CHAPTER 5

❖

ALIEN TRANSPORTER SNOT

Mitzy arrived at the vet's to find a sign on the door explaining that Dr Udall was away on holiday. But Mitzy wasn't interested in the vet. It was the multi-dimensional alien who spent her days in Dr Udall's fish bowl that Mitzy wanted to see.

"The receptionist looks after Barb when the vet is on holiday."

Mitzy turned round to find Biskit standing behind her.

"What happened to your date with a stick?" asked Mitzy.

"Nothing. It was fine. I thought I'd come and see if there was anything going on. I'm guessing there is since you want to see the fish. Come on. You can fill me in on the way over."

As Biskit led Mitzy across town, she told him what Crisp had said. Biskit listened without comment. It was unlike him to be so quiet and Mitzy wondered whether something had happened, but she didn't ask. The things that happened between a pet and their owner were no one else's business.

When they arrived at the receptionist's house, Biskit led Mitzy through a cat flap and into the living room.

It was, without doubt, the pinkest room Mitzy had ever seen. It had a pink sofa with pink scatter cushions and pink striped curtains. The wallpaper was a pink design with pink flowers. The only things that weren't pink were the frilly white doilies on the pink tablecloth.

A fish tank and a smaller bowl sat on the cabinet in front of the window. In the bowl swam Barb, a large goldfish with bulbous eyes. In the other, cowering behind an archway and some plastic seaweed, were three small pink fish, staring at Barb in absolute fear. They didn't even notice the cat enter the room.

"Hello, Biskit. Hello, Mitzy. I hate it when Dr Udall goes on holiday. This room is far too… What's the word?"

"Pink?" suggested Biskit.

"Yes. Pink." Barb did not look amused. "It's not just that. Look at these so-called tropical fish. I've met more tropical penguins on Pluto," she moaned.

"There are penguins on Pluto?" said Mitzy.

"Yes, and even they give a warmer reception than these miserable little bits of floating shark food. What do you want, anyway?"

"There's been an abduction," said Mitzy. "A rat got sneezed on by an alien, transported somewhere, then brought back again."

Barb flapped a fin, drifting up and out of the bowl with a ball of water surrounding her. The tropical fish stared in astonishment, opening and closing their mouths.

"Sounds like Snot Snatchers," said Barb.

"Snot Snatchers?" repeated Biskit.

"From Planet Bogey in the galaxy of XS Mucus," said Barb.

Biskit sniggered. "Planet Bogey."

"Laugh if you will," said Barb. "But Snot Snatchers have the most powerful snot in the universe."

"What does it do?" asked Mitzy.

"Most snot protects the body by fighting viruses and bacteria but Cosmic Snot destroys the fabric of space itself."

"Eh?" Biskit scratched his head with his paw.

Barb sighed. "The snot breaks down tiny particles that hold the universe together, meaning one can travel many light years in hardly any time at all."

"Nope. You've completely lost me." Biskit jumped on to the sofa and nestled into the soft cushion.

"She's saying they sneeze on things and transport them places," said Mitzy.

"Precisely," said Barb. "Biskit, get your muddy paws off that sofa before I give you a bath you won't forget."

Biskit climbed off the sofa. "So it's Weird Alien Transporter Snot?"

"I suppose you could call it that," said Barb with a sigh.

"Why didn't you just say that in the first place?" asked Biskit.

"The question is why would they snatch a rat?" said Mitzy.

"I have no idea," said Barb. "Funnily enough, I've never fancied visiting Planet Bogey. Something about the name. It doesn't sound like a perfect holiday destination."

"Yes, I can see why you wouldn't pick it," said Biskit with a wry smile. "Pick it? Get it?"

Barb turned to Mitzy. "It's lucky that one of you is taking this seriously."

"I get it," squeaked a small voice from behind them. They looked down to find a pink mouse with glasses and a miniature electronic tablet under his arm. "'Pick it' as in picking noses. That's the joke, isn't it? Example Six always complains that I don't get jokes but it's just that I don't find his jokes funny."

Biskit and Mitzy turned to see Example

One, the super-intelligent
lab mouse who ran
the Nothington-on-Sea
Extra-terrestrial Research
Division (or NERD, for short).
Working in the same lab where he
had once been experimented on, Example
One and his team of mice had created a
number of important inventions used by the
Pet Defenders.

Example One gazed around. "Gosh," he
said, taking in the décor. "I feel strangely at
home here."

"Where did you appear from?" asked Mitzy.

"A mouse hole," he replied. "There are
passages between all the houses in Nothington-
on-Sea. I came here to pick Barb's brains about
some interesting results I've collected on a new
invention of mine." He tapped his tablet with
the stylus and it projected a three-dimensional

holograph of Nothington-on-Sea into the middle of the room.

"What's this?" Biskit asked.

"It's a Portal Detector," said Example One. "Since learning that our town is at a structural weak point in the universe, I've been working on a device that will help us find the portals before anything comes through."

"How does it work?" asked Mitzy.

"See for yourself." Example One fiddled with the tablet again and a number of yellow circles of light appeared on the image of the town. Biskit spotted one up on Clifftop Farm where the alien dung had arrived and another outside the town hall where the Beard King had tried to bring in his army of beards through a portal. These weren't the only places he recognized. All over town he saw spots where he had encountered alien invaders, including the one in the park where he had lost Champ.

"Look, that's where Crisp said he was abducted," said Mitzy, pointing to the alley next to the fish and chip shop. "Why is it brighter than the others?"

"Because it was opened more recently," said Example One.

"This one's even brighter," said Biskit, stepping forwards to get a better view of a dot glowing as brightly as the sun.

"Yes. That one looks like it has been opened very recently," said Barb. "Possibly it is still open now. You see, the way it works—"

"Never mind that," interrupted Biskit. "Come on, Mitzy. It's in the allotments on the west side of town."

"I would advise against charging into something you don't understand," said Example One.

"We don't know how long ago the portal opened," said Barb.

"That's what we're going to find out," said Biskit. He dashed out of the door.

"Always so rash," said Example One, shaking his head. "Never thinking things through."

"All the same, I'd better go after him," said Mitzy.

"Good luck," said Barb, dropping back into the bowl with a splash.

CHAPTER 6

❧

WILD ALIEN REALITY SHOW

It was dark by the time Biskit and Mitzy arrived at the spot. Biskit nudged open a gate and followed the path that wove through the allotments. The light from the street lamps spread long shadows through the surrounding trees making the whole place feel strangely spooky.

Being so late, there were no gardeners around but Mitzy could tell from the way her partner was sniffing that they were not alone. He moved in a circle then continued in a wiggly line up the hill.

"What is it?" asked Mitzy.

"I don't know but it's not human," said Biskit.

He dropped his head again. The trail took him over rows of cabbages, parsnips, carrots and potatoes until Mitzy whispered, "Look."

A shadowy figure stood behind a small potting shed. The creature was as tall as a human, with tentacles instead of fingers. It turned and they saw a huge nose dangling from the middle of its face. The end of the nose rose up and sniffed at them.

"Ah… ah…" The alien sounded like it was about to sneeze.

"Don't even think about it, Snot Snatcher," said Biskit.

"Ah … ah…" It looked at Mitzy. "Are you dog?"

"No, I'm a cat," said Mitzy.

"Oh." Its nose flopped back down in disappointment. "Flem hoping for dog. Hard to tell what is what on this planet. You all look the same to Flem."

"I'm a dog," said Biskit.

"Really?" The alien peered at him. "Flem thought you a guinea pig."

"Guinea pig?" exclaimed Biskit.

"You are a bit guinea piggy, come to think of it," said Mitzy, winking at Biskit.

"Guinea piggy?" exploded Biskit.

"It doesn't matter." She turned to the alien. "Flem? Is that your name? We are Pet

Defenders. This is our planet and we are here to defend it."

"Flem not interested in your planet. Just need players to enter into *The WARS*."

"Wars? What wars?" said Mitzy.

"Not actual war. *WARS* stands for *Wild Alien Reality Show*," said Flem. "It's the biggest show on Planet Bogey. Flem need to pick two. Hoping one will be dog."

"Why do you want a dog?" asked Mitzy.

"That's obvious, isn't it?" said Biskit. "Dogs are the best."

"Ha," scoffed Mitzy.

"No, guinea pig is right. Flem want dog because Champ was a dog."

"I AM NOT A GUINEA… Hold on. Did you say Champ?" Biskit's ears pricked up and his nose twitched excitedly.

"Yes. Last year's best player! Flem wants dog like Champ."

"Champ? You took Champ?" Biskit barked. "What did you do to him?"

"Flem do nothing – not even snatch Champ. This Flem's first time snatching from Earth."

"You all take turns kidnapping animals from other planets? That's awful," said Mitzy.

"Awful?" replied Flem. "No. Interesting. *Wild Alien Reality Show* teaches us about wildlife of the universe. Besides, winners get very special treatment in Players' Palace."

"That's where Champ will be, then," said Biskit. "How do we get into the Players' Palace, Flem?"

"The only way is to win the show but—"

"Then that's what we'll do," interrupted Biskit.

"You mean you want to be snatched?" said Flem. "No one *ever* want to be snatched."

"If it means getting Champ back, then yes," said Biskit.

"We don't know what's up there," said Mitzy. "Our job is to keep Earth safe, not to go into space. It's too dangerous."

"I don't care," said Biskit. "I'm going. I owe it to Champ."

Mitzy had seen that look in Biskit's eyes before. It meant he had an idea in his head and nothing was going to shift it.

She turned to Flem. "Take us both," she said.

"Both of you?"

"Yes. You said you needed two. Take us both."

"Mitzy, are you sure about this?" said Biskit. "I have to go … but you don't."

"You want to find your partner," said Mitzy. "I don't want to lose mine." She turned back to face Flem. "Take us to Planet Bogey."

"OK. Flem agree. Now, stand still while I ah … ah –" the bizarre creature tipped its head back – "ah … ah … chooo!"

A stream of fluid flew out of its nose, showering Mitzy and Biskit with green goo. As it covered them, the Pet Defenders saw swirling colours appear and felt as though they were falling. It was too late to change their minds. Biskit and Mitzy were on their way to Planet Bogey.

CHAPTER 7

PLANET BOGEY

Mitzy understood what Crisp meant about it feeling like being eaten by a rainbow trapped in a tornado. Colours she didn't even know existed whizzed past her eyes. She felt herself being thrown around like a cork in the middle of an ocean. An orchestra of bizarre sounds echoed in her ears as she was transported across the universe.

A **THUD!** was followed by a sensation that felt like she was being squeezed out of a tube of toothpaste. As the gooey substance dripped away, Mitzy looked around. Biskit was next to her. He stood in a puddle of snot.

"Wow, let's do that again!" he said, shaking himself dry.

"I hate it when you do that," said Mitzy, rolling on the ground but failing to get the snot off her fur. "Where are we?"

"Some kind of sports arena, it looks like," said Biskit.

Around them stood a number of Snot Snatchers in yellow bibs. Thousands more of the strange creatures sat in stadium seats under a pale green sky.

"Look. That's Flem!" said Biskit, spotting one of the Snatchers waving frantically from a seat near the front.

In the centre of the arena stood eight other aliens. There was big-footed one with blue skin standing between a two-tailed lizard and what appeared to be a sausage with a stripy scarf. The smallest was the size of a very large insect.

"Hey. That's a Maybe Fly-mite," said Biskit, nudging Mitzy. "Not to be confused with a Might-be Mayfly. And look, there's a Flugel-horned Solar Moth over there." He indicated a moth almost the size of three elephants. "One of those tried to eat our sun once – until Champ and I convinced it that the solar flares would give it stomach ache."

"I don't recognize a thing. What's that one that looks like a cross between a skunk and a monkey?" asked Mitzy.

An alien with horns on its three heads turned to look at her. "It's called a Skumunky."

"Thanks," said Mitzy. "Hi. I'm Mitzy. This is Biskit. We're from a planet called Earth."

"Never heard of it, have we, Teds?" it replied.

"No, Ted, we haven't," said the second head.

"It's a small blue planet in a solar system known as—" began the third head.

"Shut your chatter-hole, Ted," shouted the
first two heads.

"Don't mind old three-headed Ted," said
a transparent jelly-like blob with hardly any
features except for its mouth and eyes. "He's
always arguing with himself. I'm Seema Innuds.
Me and the Teds are from a planet called

Tosting. You got snatched, too, huh?"

"Stop talking to the competition, Seema,"
said the first Ted.

"We're in this to win it," said the second.

They turned to look at the third head as
though daring him to contradict them.

"What?" said the third head. "I agree.

We shouldn't be talking. We're waiting for the last arrivals before the show can start. Oh, the final two are appearing now. Look."

Two large dollops of brightly coloured slime materialized next to Biskit. Out of one emerged what looked like a giant lobster standing on its hindlegs. Out of the other stepped a creature with four legs, two tails and an extremely long neck. It wore a distinctly snooty look on its face.

The lobster clawed its way out of the slime then made a clattering noise. **"Rring-TA-zzz-BOCK!"**

"Quite," said the long-necked alien. "An extremely poor selection of life forms. I haven't been transported halfway across the universe to rub shoulders with –" she lowered her neck to peer at Biskit – "some kind of hairy rug thing."

"I'm a dog," growled Biskit.

"Hello, *A-dog*. I am Dama Plum-ladle and this is my good friend, Mrs Sheasby the Snapper-jab. We hail from the class-one planet of Not-Nward, in the upper regions of the Galaxy of Hifalutin."

"Rring-TA-zzz-BOCK!" said the lobster.

Dama Plum-ladle laughed. "Oh, Mrs Sheasby, you're such a wit. Yes, he could do with a haircut. Now, do any of you lower life forms know what this show actually involves?"

"I think we're about to find out," said Seema.

One of the Snot Snatchers in bibs standing by the side of the arena sneezed, firing out a blob of snot with a powerful **BLAST!** The multi-coloured substance soared into the air then exploded like a firework.

"Snatchers and Snotters, welcome to the Star Stadium, here on the top of Nose Candle Mountain!"

The crowd cheered.

"Hi, everyone," added a second voice.

The voices came from a hovering platform where two grinning Snot Snatchers addressed a camera. Their faces were projected on to an enormous screen.

"I'm Hang Crusted…" said the one on the right.

"And I'm Sloop Dangler," said the other. "As usual, we're broadcasting across Planet Bogey to bring you the best show in the galaxy… *The Wild Alien Reality Show*."

The crowd whooped.

"Once again, we'll be meeting twelve fascinating species," Hang continued, "freshly snatched from six planets. All twelve will face three challenges…"

"While trying to avoid getting gunged by the gunge-bots," added Sloop.

The contestants looked up to see a number of metal noses flying over the auditorium.

"Gunge them! Gunge them!" cried the crowd, honking their noses and firing bursts of snot into the air.

"Yes," said Hang. "The losers will spend the rest of the show in the gunge dungeons where all the waste snot from the Star Stadium collects. After that, they'll be moved to Snot City High-security Alien Zoo…"

"Now, there's a great day out for the little snifflers," said Sloop. "And only a short stroll from Big Sneeze Falls and the Players' Palace…"

"… where the winners get to live a life of luxury with everything they desire," said Hang.

"Luckily I have everything I desire right here," said Sloop with a big cheesy grin.

"Because this is *The Wild Alien Reality Show* and it's about to begin."

A Snot Snatcher standing by the side of the arena in a green bib blew a fanfare with its nose. The crowd went wild and the commentators continued.

"Up first, from the planet Kitch, we have a Juggle-throttled Bull Sniffler and a Dandy Crawler," said Hang. "We've had both species before … but never together. And look over there. We've gotta couple of Earth creatures. Let's see now. We appear to have a domestic feline, otherwise known as a cat. And what's that with it?"

"Some kind of large gerbil, I think, Hang?"

"I'm a dog," barked Biskit. But the commentators weren't listening – they were continuing to introduce the contestants.

"Now, using the latest Snot-nology we

scanned the brains of our players while they were transported here. And we'll be using all the information gathered to get the best out of them."

"That's right, Hang. They will literally come face to face with their biggest fears," said Sloop. "Bogey-licious, eh?"

"It sounds awful," said Mitzy with a shudder.

"I'm not worried," said Biskit. "I don't fear anything."

"Everyone is scared of something," said Ted's first head.

"Even us," said the second head.

"My greatest fear is having to spend the rest of my life listening to you two," said the third head. "No, wait a minute, that's my actual life."

"You think you're so smart," said the first.

"Yeah," said the second. "You're not though."

Ted's third head rolled his eyes. "Oh, go knock your heads together, Teds."

"'Scuse me, Earth cat," said Seema. "I don't think I have a brain, do I? Can you see a brain in here?"

Mitzy could see nothing but transparent jelly behind Seema's eyes but she didn't want to be unkind. "I'm sure it's there somewhere," she said.

"Thanks," said Seema. "But I'm not bothered really. Brains are overrated, if you ask me. No one does, though. I suppose because I don't have one."

Dama Plum-ladle lowered her long neck and peered at Seema. "Those without brains should do us all a favour and remain quiet."

"Rring-TA-zzz-BOCK!" said the large lobster.

Dama Plum-ladle hooted with laughter. "Oh, Mrs Sheasby, that's very amusing. You are so very droll."

"And now we've met our contestants…" Hang's voice echoed off the stadium walls. "It's time for Round One."

CHAPTER 8

ROUND ONE: FOOD OF FEAR

The crowd of Snot Snatchers and the contestants listened as the commentators introduced the first round.

"The rules are simple," said Hang. "Each player must find their place at the table being set by our stewards and consume the meal that has been specially prepared for them."

A number of Snot Snatchers in green bibs carried in a long table upon which they placed twelve metal bowls.

Hang continued. "The first six contestants to finish will go through to the next round."

"Eating food?" said Biskit. "Now that I can do. I haven't eaten since breakfast."

"It's too easy," said Mitzy. "There must be more to it."

"Oh, there's one more thing," said Hang. "Each bowl will contain the player's worst food nightmare."

"You mean the one thing they hate eating the most?" said Sloop.

"You got it," said Hang. "So, players, on your marks … get set … eat!"

A Snot Snatcher at the side of the arena made a loud tooting noise and the odd assortment of aliens walked, crawled, slithered or flew towards the table to find the place marked with their name. Biskit found his between the sausage in a scarf and three-headed Ted.

Ted removed the lid of his platter and all three of his heads peered into his bowl.

"What is it?" asked the first head.

"Oh no. It's Yucky-splung soup," said the second. "I hate Yucky-splung soup."

"Of course we hate it," snapped the third. "That's the point. Come on. I'm not eating it all on my own." He lifted a spoon and tasted it. "Eurgh. It's not even warm."

Ted picked up two more spoons, which he lifted to the other two heads. The first shuddered as he tasted the stuff while the second pulled such a horrified face that the crowd exploded with laughter at the image of it on the large screen.

Next to him, Seema was guzzling its meal down, eating straight from the bowl.

"Hold on," said Ted's second head. "Isn't it supposed to be a meal you hate?"

Seema looked up from the bowl. "No taste buds." Sludgy goo dribbled down its chin, drawing yet more laughter from the crowd.

Biskit nudged the lid off his bowl. It appeared to be a rather tasty-looking pie. "Ha, told you!" he said. "I'm not scared of anything. I love pies!"

The commentators gave a running commentary for the crowd.

"Some good reactions so far," said Hang.

"It's gunge-alicious," said Sloop. "What's the Snapper-jab got?"

"Some kind of maggot stew," said Hang.

"Ew," said Sloop. "That's not my cup of snot tea for sure."

"Rring-TA-zzz-BOCK!" The Snapper-jab was refusing to go near the bowl.

"Now, Mrs Sheasby, you simply must eat your food," said Dama Plum-ladle.

Mrs Sheasby gave her usual clattering response.

"Rring-TA-zzz-BOCK!"

"Yes but the rules are clear. We must eat and eat quickly if we are to avoid being gunged. Do you think I am enjoying this plate of shredded worm entrails? No, I am not – but I am eating them none the less."

"Rring-TA-zzz-BOCK!" Mrs Sheasby kicked over her bowl defiantly.

The crowd gasped and she turned to snarl at them.

The crowd booed, blew their noses angrily and chanted, "Gunge! Gunge! Gunge!"

"Looks like we might have our first victim," said Sloop.

"Time to send in a gunge-bot!" replied Hang.

One of the flying noses swooped down over

Mrs Sheasby's head.

"Gunge! Gunge! Gunge!" bayed the crowd.

The lobster tried to scuttle away but the gunge-bot followed her and dropped its load of thick green liquid. The other players stopped and stared as Mrs Sheasby was covered in slime. The Cosmic Snot glowed and turned a hundred different colours in a second before Mrs Sheasby vanished.

"What a shame," said Dama Plum-ladle. "Still, if you will be a picky eater…"

"And so the gunge-bots claim their first victim," said Hang's voice over the loudspeaker. "The Snapper-jab goes down to the dungeon."

"She'll be joined by five more from this round," said Sloop, "so you'd better get eating!"

"He's right, Mitzy," said Biskit. "What have you got?"

"Mushrooms," said Mitzy miserably.

"That's not so bad," said Biskit. "Philip's

ex-girlfriend, Susie, used to make a lovely mushroom Wellington. Yum."

"It's not only the taste," said Mitzy. "It's the effect they have on me."

"What does that mean?" asked Biskit.

Mitzy lowered her voice. "Let's just say they come out quicker than they go in."

"Oh, I see," said Biskit.

All around the table, the other players were eating as fast as they could manage, wincing, choking and moaning as they forced the food into their mouths. On the far side of the table, the Solar Moth had an extreme allergic reaction to its meal, resulting in an explosion of warts. The crowd found it all hilarious.

Mitzy tried to cover her nose as she ate her bowl of mushrooms and Biskit tried to figure out why the Snot Snatchers thought he hated pumpkin pie. It was delicious. But as he munched his way through it, he found the taste awakened a memory. Susie had made this pie the night she told Philip she was leaving.

As Biskit remembered that awful night, he forgot all about the competition – he forgot everything except the feeling of helplessness and that somehow it was his fault. He was so lost in this sad memory that it was a surprise to hear Hang say, "It looks like we have our first crier."

"Let's hear a big 'Ahh!' for the Earth squirrel," said Sloop.

"I'm … a … dog," Biskit muttered between his sobs.

"Mind you, it looks like the cat's meal is already on its way out," said Hang.

"Let's get a big 'Eurgh!' for the Earth cat," said Sloop. "But at least both Earth players have finished their meals and are through to the next round!"

CHAPTER 9

ROUND TWO: THE WALK OF FEAR

The stewards divided the remaining six players into two teams of three. Biskit, Mitzy and three-headed Ted stood on one side of the arena while Dama Plum-ladle, Seema and the Skumunky waited on the other.

Hang addressed the crowd. "Snatchers and Snotters, let's remind ourselves who's left. We have the Wibble-drobbler and the Tri-headed Affle-waffler from the planet Holden."

The crowd cheered for three-headed Ted and Seema.

"The Skumunky from the planet Galvin,

the Long-necked Hoofler from the planet Not-Nwod…"

"It's Not-Nward actually," proclaimed Dama Plum-ladle.

"And last but not least, our pair from Earth, the cat…."

The biggest cheer yet went up.

"And the… What is that again? A koala?"

"No, I think it's some kind of burrowing creature," said Sloop.

"I just wish they'd get it into their stupid noses that I'm a dog," said Biskit.

The stewards were busy setting up the next round, which appeared to involve three long thin poles running from one side of the arena to the other, a couple of metres off the ground.

"Maybe it's some kind of assault course," said Biskit. "I hope so. I'm great at assault courses."

"Always so modest," said Mitzy with a wink.

A Snot Snatcher trumpeted his nose to get

the crowd's attention, then Hang continued. "And so to Round Two, The Walk of Fear. Once again, the rules couldn't be simpler. Each contestant must make it to the other side of the pole without touching the ground."

"But hang on, Hang," said Sloop. "There are six contestants but only three poles."

"That's right, Sloop. Each player will have to pass another to reach the end. If they can pass each other without falling, both go through to the next round but if they both fall, they're both out. Now, players, take your places!"

Biskit jumped up on to the pole and saw Dama Plum-ladle at the other end. Mitzy hopped on to a pole with Seema at the other, while three-headed Ted faced the Skumunky.

"Oh, great," said Ted's first head. "We get Mister Smelly."

"It's revolting," said his second head.

"I think it can hear us," said Ted's third head.

The starting toot sounded and the six players began to edge forwards. Biskit took a couple of cautious steps, only to discover that the pole was covered in a thin layer of slime. As all the players fought to keep their balance, the audience rocked with laughter and hooted hysterically.

Under normal circumstances, Mitzy would have reached the other end of the pole in a flash but Seema was so wobbly that the pole rocked dangerously.

"Look at them go," said Hang. "What great players."

"And a fantastic audience," said Sloop. "Maybe it's time to give them something to do."

"Good idea," said Hang. "Snotters and Snatchers, please PICK YOUR BOGEYS."

"I've got a bad feeling about this," muttered Mitzy under her breath. She was moving steadily but carefully towards Seema, who was slowly shifting along the pole towards her.

"Yes, folks, everyone in the audience has been given one Cosmic Snot Ball," said Hang. "Each bogey is charged with Cosmic Terror-snot."

"Maybe you could explain that for the viewers at home," said Sloop.

"Certainly, Sloop. Cosmic Terror-snot awakens a deeply held fear in its target."

"That's it. The only thing to fear is fear itself … and bogeys!" said Sloop.

"Snatchers and Snotters, get flicking!" cried Hang.

Suddenly the air was full of bogeys the size
of tennis balls. The huge blobs of snot rained
down on the players. Biskit jumped to avoid
one, only to feel another hit him right between
the eyes. He wobbled but managed to stay
on the pole, shaking his head to get rid of the
slimy substance. When he opened his eyes he
saw that the ground beneath him had vanished.
Below him was nothing but endless star-filled
space. He felt a lurch of terror in his stomach
and his legs went wobbly.

Biskit shook his head. He knew it was just a trick. He crouched down and clung on tightly as another bogey hit him. This time, the Cosmic Snot sent his thoughts whirling back to Philip. The last time he had seen him, they had argued and he'd run off. He felt a sudden surge of panic about what would happen if he never made it back to Earth. Philip would be left thinking that he had run off, just like Champ's owners did.

Biskit felt more bogeys pummel his head and body, each one bringing with it a new fear, more troubling than the previous one. He knew the only way to get through was to keep moving and so he kept his head down and edged along the poll, teeth gritted, eyes shut.

CHAPTER 10

THE FEELING OF FEELINGS

Mitzy was nimbly avoiding the flying bogeys, while they were passing straight through Seema and dropping out the other side. Remarkably, the jelly-like creature was keeping its balance. Rolls of transparent flab flopped over the side of the pole, leaving no room for Mitzy to squeeze past.

"Seema, what happens when the bogeys hit you?" she asked.

"I wouldn't know," said Seema. "I've got no feelings."

"What? You can't feel anything?" said Mitzy.

"I don't know. What does feeling feel like?"

"Feeling feels like ... well, feeling." Mitzy avoided a bogey aimed at her head then span round to dodge three more. She landed in front of Seema. She teetered and almost lost her balance but Seema didn't slow down. Mitzy tried to jump back but discovered her tail was trapped under the weight of the alien.

"Seema," she yelled. "Stop!"

"Sorry. I'll topple if I stop moving forwards."

Mitzy ducked down. She had no choice but to allow the huge wobbling bulk to pass over her back.

The cheers of the crowd sounded muffled and everything looked warped and misshapen from under Seema's belly.

"Look at that," said Sloop. "The Wibble-drobbler is passing over the Earth cat."

"Yes, this big wobbling mass of alien might not look like much of a contender," said Hang. "But just look how the Cosmic Terror-snot bogeys are passing straight through it."

"Right on to the Earth cat by the looks of things," said Hang.

As a bogey came out through Seema, it squished into Mitzy's back and the Cosmic Terror-snot took effect. Suddenly she was alone. Everyone had gone. Seema, the other players, the stewards, the commentators, gunge-bots, camera-bots and the audience had all vanished.

"Hello?" she called. "Where is everyone?"

No one responded.

Mitzy clung on to the pole and closed her eyes. Even though she could no longer see the audience lobbing the bogeys at her, they continued to hit her and every one of them brought with it a sad memory or an unsettling thought.

She was transported back to the day she had returned home to find Cynthia gone. Her owner had left no explanation, just an empty house. Mitzy had been so sure Cynthia would come back, she had waited for a week. It had been the worst week of her life. At least life on the streets involved other animals. Stuck in the house, it had been just her.

Mitzy fought against these bad thoughts but each time one faded, another bogey hit her and brought a fresh fear. Mitzy carried on moving, struggling against the onslaught. When she reached the other side and stepped back on to solid ground, she heard the roar of the crowd as everything reappeared in front of her eyes.

She turned round to see that Seema had fallen off the pole.

Three-headed Ted, who was level with Mitzy but heading in the other direction, saw this and laughed.

"What a fool," said Ted's first head.

"Brainless idiot," said the second.

"Er, Teds, you might want to keep an eye on our opponent," said the third.

The other two heads turned as the Skumunky sprang up on to Ted's shoulders, releasing a yellow gas with such a disgusting smell that Ted fell off the pole and was instantly gunged.

"The Skumunky and the Earth cat get through to the final round," announced Hang. "But will the Long-necked Hoofler get the better of the … er…"

"Whatever it is, it looks like we have a good

old-fashioned stand off, Hang," said Sloop.

By now the crowd had run out of bogeys to throw. With the other contestants finished, everyone's attention was on Biskit and Dama Plum-ladle.

"Why don't you do us all a favour and just jump awf?" said Dama Plum-ladle.

She swung her neck at Biskit but he jumped out of the way just in time.

"Sticking your neck out, eh?" said Biskit, regaining his balance on the pole.

"I find neck comments extremely offensive. I'll have you know, I am a highly evolved species."

"Yes, you stand head and shoulders above me," said Biskit. "Unfortunately for you that is not always an advantage."

Without warning, Biskit ran forwards, knocking the alien's legs and sending her flying. As a gunge-bot dropped its load on her, the crowd went wild, their cheers getting even louder as Biskit reached the other side.

"And so we have our three finalists," said Hang. "Meaning it is time to move on to our third and final round."

CHAPTER 11

·:·

ROUND THREE: FEAR BEASTS

The centre of the arena felt much larger now that Mitzy, Biskit and the Skumunky were the only ones left in the competition.

"What a show," said Hang.

"Bogey-dacious!" added Sloop. The crowd laughed. "A pair of Earth players make it to the final round for the second year running."

"And we all remember what happened in last year's final, Hang…"

"Never mind last year," said Hang quickly. "Snotters and Snatchers, it's time for Round Three."

"So what happens in this round, Hang?" said Sloop.

"I'm glad you asked, Sloop," said Hang. "Round Three is the big one. Fear Beasts."

"Fear Beasts?" said Sloop. "Tell us more."

"Our top team of Snot Snatchers have travelled the universe to collect the creatures feared the most by each player."

"Sounds pretty scary," said Sloop.

"Let's hope so." Hang laughed. "The winner will be the first player to defeat his or her Fear Beast. So, without further ado, let's meet the monsters."

The lights dimmed and the stadium was filled with the sound of honking noses and stamping feet as three huge creatures appeared in a glowing **FLA-DASH!** of Cosmic Snot. Each one appeared in front of the player it was supposed to fight.

"They're here," Hang's voice boomed.

"They're about to get near," said Sloop.

"And it's your worst fear!" added Hang. "Snotters and Snatchers, it's the FEAR BEASTS!"

Biskit's was the first to emerge from its gunky cocoon. It was the size of a small hill with fists like a gorilla and a shark fin on its back. It turned its head to look at Biskit.

"What is that?" asked Mitzy.

"It's an Aqua-grilla. I haven't seen one of those in a long time, which is more than I can say for yours. That's a Dung Guzzler, the first alien we fought together."

An enormous beetle clawed its way from its coat of snot and turned its huge glassy eyes to look at Mitzy. It clashed its claws together and they fizzled with purple bolts of electricity.

"I know what it is," said Mitzy.

"That's the thing you're most scared of?" Biskit asked.

"Yes. So what?" said Mitzy.

"I mean, I know it was scary but—"

Biskit was cut off by a ground-shaking thump from the Aqua-grilla.

Oruuuga-snap-snap! growled the terrifying creature, swinging its other fist at him. Biskit rolled out of reach while Mitzy was zigzagging away from the Dung Guzzler's claws.

On the other side of the arena, the Skumunky had been cornered by its Fear Beast, a gigantic sabretoothed snake. A cloud of stinky gas surrounded the Skumunky but its defensive smell was having no effect on the beast.

"It seems our Skumunky's Fear Beast, the Keema, has no nose," said Hang.

"No nose? Really?" asked Sloop. "How does it smell?"

"It can't smell, Sloop. That's the point," said Hang.

The Keema opened its jaws and was about to swallow the Skumunky whole when two gunge-bots flew overhead, dropped their load, and transported them both away. The crowd went wild with honking applause.

"Bye bye, Skumunky," said Hang.

"Smell you later," added Sloop.

"And it's a one-planet final," said Hang.

"Looks as though the cat might be the next

one to bite the dust," replied Sloop.

Mitzy knew it couldn't be the same beetle she and Biskit had blown to pieces back on Earth but it certainly seemed to have it in for her.

"Listen," she said. "Maybe we could talk about this. I'm not really your enemy here."

Scrikerty-tick-tick came the sound of the beetle as it brought its claws together, sending bolts of purple electricity flying. Mitzy dived out of the way.

Oruuuga-snap-snap! grunted the Aqua-grilla as it swung an enormous hand at Biskit. He could hear the honking applause of the crowd. He didn't know if they were egging him on or cheering for his opponent.

He rolled out of the way and sprang back to his feet. Watching a jet of water shoot out of a blowhole in the Aqua-grilla's back, Biskit was transported back to the last time he had come face to face with the creature.

It had been his first-ever mission as a Pet Defenders agent. Biskit had tried to impress his partner, Champ, and had almost got them both killed. These thoughts filled his mind as he dodged, dived and ducked out of the way of the creature while it chased him around the arena. Biskit had fought bigger and scarier things since meeting the Aqua-grilla but, seeing it again, he felt like the same nervous rookie he had been back then.

Oruuuga-snap-snap! Another jet of water rained down on Biskit. He shook his fur dry angrily and snarled, "Right, that's it. Enough snot and bogeys and … I don't even want to know what that was."

Oruuuga-snap-snap! The lumbering beast brought its powerful fist down millimetres away from his nose. Biskit skidded to a halt and changed direction. He could see Mitzy running the other way, closely pursued by the Dung Guzzler.

"It looks like our remaining players are heading for a collision," said Hang.

"This is gonna be crash-tastic," said Sloop.

"A collision. That's it," muttered Biskit to himself. "Mitzy," he barked. "We need to introduce that Dung Guzzler to this Aqua-grilla."

"Really?" cried Mitzy, who was having enough of a problem with one Fear Beast without adding another.

"Yes, I've got a feeling sparks will fly," yelled Biskit.

"Sparks. Yes!"

"Ready... Run!"

Biskit and Mitzy kept to the edge of the arena, each moving in opposite directions.

The crowd was going crazy, cheering and shouting. The Aqua-grilla snapped its jaws at Biskit, catching a couple of tail hairs. Then, just as the Pet Defenders were about to collide,

Mitzy backflipped and slid into the centre of the arena, under the Dung Guzzler's belly, while Biskit took a skidding right turn. The Aqua-grilla twisted round to grab him but the beetle's claws closed round the Aqua-grilla's throat.

Oruuuga-snap-snap!
Scrikerty-tick-tick!

The Aqua-grilla shot a jet of water that rained down on the beetle's back. Instantly, purple sparks few everywhere as the creature came into contact with to the gushing water.

Oruuuga-snap-snap!

Scrikerty-tick-tick!

Vvvvvooo-WHOOO-BANG!

The crowd gasped as the beetle exploded.

The force of the blast made the entire stadium rock and the Aqua-grilla collapsed to the ground.

Mitzy and Biskit emerged from the rubble, covered in bits of exploded beetle.

"KABOOM!" cried Sloop. "What a night! What a contest! What a show!"

"You can say that again," said Hang. "In a final reminiscent of last year, the Earthlings have both defeated their Fear Beasts."

"So what happens now, Hang?" asked Sloop,

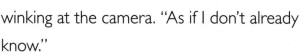

winking at the camera. "As if I don't already know."

"Now they have to fight each other to see who will go to the Players' Palace," said Hang.

"That's right, folks," said Sloop. "There can only be one winner. One's going to the Players' Palace, the other is gonna get…"

Sloop paused and waited for the crowd to yell, "GUNGED!"

Hang laughed. "Yes, the winner will have to hold his opponent down for a full round of nose blows from our officials."

Mitzy lowered her head and spoke in a whisper. "You should win," she said. "If Champ is in the Players' Palace, you should be the one to find him."

"No," said Biskit. "It's my fault we're here. I should be the one to get gunged."

"But—"

"Mitzy, I'm the senior agent. This is my call.

Now, watch it."

"Watch what?"

"Me." Biskit suddenly lunged at her.

Mitzy tried to jump out of the way but Biskit rolled over and knocked her legs so she fell on top of him.

"Biskit, stop it." Mitzy struggled to get free.

"Hold still," muttered Biskit, "they're sneezing."

Around the side of the arena the Snatchers in bibs began to blow their noses, one at a time.

"I hope you know what you're doing," said Mitzy.

"Yes, I'm putting my partner first," said Biskit. "Get into the Players' Palace, find Champ and bring him home."

With each hoot, the crowd grew increasingly excited until the final nose blew and they erupted into a thunderous round of applause.

"Snatchers and Snotters, it's all over," Hang

cried. "The cat from Earth defeats her planet partner and becomes this year's *Wild Alien Reality Show* winner."

Mitzy couldn't help but smile as the crowd cheered and chanted, "Earth cat! Earth cat!" She looked at Biskit, lying still on the ground. He winked.

"And let's not forget our runner-up, the … er … other Earth inhabitant."

"Dog," muttered Biskit. "I'm a—"

A shadow fell over him as a gunge-bot appeared over his head.

"Find Champ," he said as the gunge rained down on him.

CHAPTER 12

THE GUNGE DUNGEON

The Cosmic Snot dripped off Biskit's fur into a pool of green sludge. He looked at his surroundings. He had been transported into a large cave-like room with the ten other players.

"Oh, it's you, is it?" said Dama Plum-ladle.

"Rring-TA-zzz-BOCK!" said Mrs Sheasby.

"Oh, Mrs Sheasby, I don't know how you keep your sense of humour in this place."

The Solar Moth folded its wings over its head to shield itself from the constant drizzle of slime while the Maybe Fly-mite was doing backstroke through the sludge. Three-headed

Ted sat miserably in a corner, with all three heads bowed.

"It's revolting down here," said his first head.

"Really disgusting," said the second.

"I blame you two for this," said the third.

"Us?" said the first. "It was you who tipped us off balance."

"I blame Seema," said the second.

"Me? What did I do?" responded Seema, opening its mouth wide and catching the snot so that it dribbled down through its see-through body.

"Never mind," said Biskit. "There's no point arguing with each other … or yourself. If we're going to get out of here, we all need to work together."

Dama Plum-ladle's neck wobbled as she laughed mockingly. "You ridiculous creature. There's no getting out."

"There's always a way out," said Biskit.

"Not from here," said Ted's first head.

"These dungeons are built to contain the waste snot," said his second.

"It comes in through these tiny holes," said his third, pointing at where a trickle of slime came dripping through the ceiling. "But we've checked. There are no doors and no windows."

"Yes, we are trapped until those vile creatures move us to the zoo to be displayed like wild animals," said Dama Plum-ladle.

"Rring-TA-zzz-BOCK!" said Mrs Sheasby.

"Well, quite." Dama Plum-ladle nodded at the huge lobster.

Biskit felt the fresh lump of gunge dribble off the end of his nose and he sat down with a squelch, miserably wondering whether he'd made the right decision.

Meanwhile, Mitzy had been transported to a sparkling silvery hallway with a long white staircase and hundreds of doors.

"Hello?" she called.

No one replied. Mitzy took a couple of cautious steps up the staircase. There was something extremely peaceful about the place. At the top of the staircase she saw an open door. She stepped inside to find a comfy sofa under the glow of a soft lamp.

As she approached she spotted a bowl full of food. She sniffed the contents and knew instantly what it was: Meow Chow's Turkey Special freshly forked from the tin. Her absolute favourite. Unable to resist, she gulped it down in a matter of seconds. Once her stomach was satisfyingly full, she scratched the side of the sofa, then sprang up on to it and curled up. All thoughts of Biskit, the show and Champ began to fade as she felt a warm sleepy feeling spread over her.

Then she heard a voice. "Mitzy? It *is* you. I was watching that awful show of theirs! I can't believe it's actually you."

Mitzy lifted her heavy eyelids and saw a human face she knew extremely well.

"Cynthia?" meowed Mitzy.

"Mitzy, my dear puss," replied Mitzy's elderly owner.

For a moment, Mitzy considered that this could be some kind of trick but she knew Cynthia well enough to know the truth.

Her scent, the look in her eyes and that loving smile all belonged to the real Cynthia.

"I've missed you so much, my little one," she said.

She picked up Mitzy and nuzzled her nose into her back. After all this time, Mitzy finally felt as though she was home.

CHAPTER 13

·:·

DOWN THE DRAIN

Mitzy wished the cuddle would never end.

"I suppose those awful snotty aliens took you, too, did they?" said Cynthia, stroking Mitzy just behind the ears. "What a terrible contest. I would never have got through it if it hadn't been for Champ. What a dog."

The name jolted Mitzy out of her hazy dreamlike state and she remembered what she was supposed to be doing.

"Oh, he was a lovely thing," continued Cynthia. "Quite remarkable, too. He got me through every round and then, just before we were supposed to fight each other, he vanished and they made me the winner. Fancy that!"

Mitzy remembered Biskit's sacrifice.

"It's funny because I've always been more of a cat person," said Cynthia. "But you know that, of course."

"Champ didn't win?" Mitzy knew full well that Cynthia couldn't understand her but that had never stopped her saying how she felt. Sometimes she wondered if Cynthia could follow what she was saying, although this wasn't one of those occasions.

"Yes, I've missed you, too," said Cynthia.

"I have to go." Mitzy desperately wanted to make Cynthia understand. "I have to find Biskit and tell him." She jumped down.

"Where are you going, Mitzy?" said Cynthia.

Mitzy scratched at the door and Cynthia pulled it open for her. "That's the wonderful thing about this place. You can do anything you want. My knees don't even hurt here. It's quite miraculous."

Mitzy padded down the steps and nudged open the front door.

"Oh, I see," said Cynthia. "You want to go home."

"Yes," Mitzy meowed sadly.

"But, you see, there's nothing for me there," said Cynthia. "Nothing except a retirement home full of other old people. On this planet, I can have everything I ever wanted. There are lots of interesting folk that live here. I can even understand some of them. I have a lovely natter every morning with a Bottopotamus from a place called Bomping Flex … wherever that is. And this planet is actually rather beautiful … once you've got over the whole snot business. I'm happy here. Especially now I've got you, my beautiful puss."

Mitzy looked up into her owner's loving eyes. All this time she had spent looking for Cynthia and now she had to leave her. The Players' Palace may have been the perfect place for Cynthia to retire but Mitzy still had a job to do.

"Cynthia," she said, stretching out her front legs and arching her back. "I know you can't understand me but I need to tell you this anyway. You will always be my owner. I am your cat and I want you to know how glad I am that you've found a place you're happy, but I can't stay on this planet. I have a job to do and I have a partner relying on me."

"There there, puss," said Cynthia. "Don't worry about me. I'm happy here. You go and do whatever you have to do. You know where to find me."

After a final cuddle and a stroke, Mitzy wriggled free from Cynthia's embrace and walked out.

Down in the gunge dungeon, Biskit was miserably watching the aliens argue.

"Mother was right," said Ted's first head. "You two have always held me back."

"Yeah, that's right. Hold on. *Us* two? What did I do?" asked head number two.

"Will you two keep it down?" said the third head. "I'm trying to sleep, which is hard enough while one is knee-deep in gunge."

"Knee-deep." Biskit's ears pricked up. "That's it!"

"What's what?" asked Seema.

"This stuff has stayed the same depth since we got here," replied Biskit.

"Oh, how fascinating," said Dama Plum-ladle,

stifling a yawn.

"We'll never get home," wailed the sausage in the stripy scarf.

"But don't you see?" said Biskit. "If the level isn't rising, it must be going somewhere. The question is – where's the drain?"

"Very interesting," said Dama Plum-ladle sarcastically.

"Actually, I think he has a point," said Ted's third head. "Where is the snot going?"

"Oh, you mean the drain in the corner of the room?" said Seema.

Everyone turned to look at the jelly-like alien.

"What? Why are all you staring like that?" it asked.

"What drain?" asked Biskit.

"It's over in that corner. I kept getting stuck in it. I hate drains. We lost my uncle down one."

"And you didn't think to tell anyone?" said Ted's first head.

"About my uncle?" said Seema.

"About the drain," said the second head.

"Nope," said Seema. "No brain, see?"

Biskit waded over to the corner of the room until he felt ridges beneath his feet. He plunged his head into the pool. It was disgusting. He opened his mouth and tried to get a grip on the grate. *It's just custard*, he thought. *Yes, a big bowl of lovely custard. Lovely … green … smelly custard.* Biskit couldn't take it any more. He raised his head and gasped for breath.

"I can't do it," he said. "I can't get a good enough grip."

"Rring-TA-zzz-BOCK!"

"Yes, I suppose they are, Mrs Sheasby." Dama Plum-ladle turned to address Biskit. "Mrs Sheasby has pointed out that her claws are ideal for such a job."

The lobster waded across to join Biskit then

thrust her claws into the pool and yanked, pulling the grate out. Instantly the thick liquid that filled the room began to swirl.

"Is this wise?" asked Ted's first head.

"Yes, we don't even know where that goes," said the second.

"Couldn't be any worse than here," said the third.

"Exactly," said Biskit. "Here goes nothing."

Biskit dived head first into the swirling whirlpool of goo.

CHAPTER 14

🐾

AN EXCLUSIVE INTERVIEW

Leaving the Players' Palace wasn't hard at all. All Mitzy had to do was nudge open the door and walk out. And yet those steps away from Cynthia were the hardest she had ever taken.

She stopped on the doorstep and looked out at the alien landscape. Strangely shaped bottle-green plants grew out of the muddy green ground. Mint-coloured clouds crossed a pale green sky. A dark green gunge-river ran down a mountainside then crashed over a cliff's edge, forming a slow-moving waterfall.

Hang Crusted and Sloop Dangler stood in

front of the waterfall, talking to a camera-bot. Mitzy crept up behind them to hear what they were saying.

"We're here at the foot of Big Sneeze Falls, a bogey's throw from the Players' Palace, to take a look back over some of the highlights from this year's *Wild Alien Reality Show*," said Hang.

"What a show it was, Hang," said Sloop. "It was phlegm-tastic!"

"It was what?" Mitzy was unable to contain herself. "You think it's good to snatch aliens from their home planets, bring them here, then put them through all that horrible stuff?"

Hang and Sloop turned to look at her.

"Snotters and Snatchers," said Hang, with a sideways wink to the camera. "We have an exclusive interview with this year's winner, the Earth cat."

"Mitzy," said Mitzy angrily. "My name is Mitzy."

"Well, Mitzy, thanks for a terrific show."

Hang draped a tentacle round her neck. "You've got a lot of fans out there."

"I don't care about your stupid game show," said Mitzy.

Sloop gasped. "Stupid?"

"Game show?" said Hang. "*The Wild Alien Reality Show* is an entertaining way of learning about all the interesting life in the universe."

"What do you learn from making us face our worst fears, fight our worst enemies and then our best friends? Not to mention the –" Mitzy could barely bring herself to say it – "mushrooms."

Hang hesitated. "I, er… Well, we learn how different species behave. Like now, who would have guessed that you would walk straight out of the Players' Palace in order to give us an exclusive interview?"

"That's not why I'm here." Mitzy felt frustrated. She knew she had to find a way off the planet but she also wanted to convince the Snatchers to stop playing their game.

"So why are you here?" asked Hang.

"I'm here to…" Mitzy raised a leg and began cleaning it with her tongue. The layers of snot and slime covering her felt revolting. "I'm here to…"

Her words trailed away as she spotted something. A familiar ball of brown fluff was moving down the side of the mountain, bobbing along the gunge-river.

"Biskit?" cried Mitzy. "Biskit!"

He was heading for the waterfall and he wasn't the only one. All of the other contestants were behind him. She could see the enormous moth trying to escape the river but the gunge was too sticky. None of them could escape as it dragged them down towards the sudden drop.

"This is just in, folks," said Hang. "The players have escaped the gunge dungeon. The drama never stops with this competition."

"And now they're heading for a snot-tacular fall," said Sloop.

"Biskit!" Mitzy yelled. "Watch out. There's a waterfall."

"Don't worry," said Sloop, "With the soft consistency of the snot and the low gravity of our planet, there is no danger."

"I hope you're right," said Mitzy as Biskit flew over the edge of the cliff and dropped into the pool below.

CHAPTER 15

🐾

THE BISKIT SHOW

Biskit didn't spot the waterfall until he was flying over it. He could see the others flailing around behind him but he had no time to warn them. As he fell, he wondered if the gravity on Planet Bogey was making the fall last longer than normal or if the Cosmic Snot was affecting his mind. All he could think about was putting things right with Philip. He had to get back to Earth.

Down in the frothing pool of snot he doggy-paddled to the side and climbed out to find Hang and Sloop waiting for him. Mitzy helped him up on to the riverbank.

"Thanks," he said.

"It's good to see you…" she replied.

He shook himself dry, showering all three of them in green goo.

"… although I could do without the snot showers," Mitzy said with a shudder.

Biskit grinned sheepishly. "Sorry. So where's Champ?"

"I don't know," admitted Mitzy.

"You're looking for Champ?" said Hang.

"Yes, that's why we're here," said Biskit.

"No one knows where he is," said Hang.

"What?" said Biskit.

"He disappeared," said Sloop. "He got down to the final then just vanished."

"What do you mean he vanished?" said Biskit.

"One minute he was there in the final, the next he had gone," said Sloop. "So we had to make that old human the winner."

"No one saw that coming. What a terrific

end to a show," said Hang. "We should get another dog next year. Don't suppose you know any good dogs, do you?" he asked.

"I'm a dog!" yelped Biskit. "I'm a dog. I am a dog. Get it into your stupid long noses that I AM A DOG!"

"You're a dog?" said Hang.

"YES!"

"But you don't look like Champ," said Sloop.

"If you knew anything about our planet, you'd know that dogs come in all shapes and sizes," said Biskit. "One of which is mine."

"Of course!" said Mitzy. "That's what you should be doing – not putting on this silly show."

"Silly?" said Hang. "Hold on. Cut the camera. Stop filming."

The green light on the camera went off and Hang turned to Mitzy. "Learning about other species isn't silly."

"No … but instead of snatching aliens,

you should be observing them."

"*What?*" said Sloop.

"You Snot Snatchers have the most amazing ability," Mitzy explained. "You can transport yourself across the universe in no time at all but you waste it on nonsense."

"Nonsense?" said Sloop.

"Yes," said Mitzy firmly. "You call it a reality show but there's nothing real about it."

"Not real?" said Hang. "Of course it's real. Real aliens. Real stadium. Real fear."

"But that's not our real life, is it?" said Mitzy.

"Where's the drama in real life? Where's the excitement?" asked Hang.

"Where's the fun?" added Sloop.

"We're Pet Defenders," said Biskit. "We've got more drama and excitement than all of your shows put together. If you want to make a really good reality show, you should be watching us."

"I didn't mean watching *us* necessarily," said Mitzy, frowning.

"Wait a minute, this is an interesting idea," said Hang, turning to the camera-bot. "Coming soon, from the team behind *The Wild Alien Reality Show*, a new kind of show … *The Wild Alien* Real *Reality Show*."

"Or even better, *The Biskit Show*," said Biskit.

Mitzy threw him a withering glance. "The point is you don't have to snatch anyone. You can just watch them."

"I like it," said Sloop. "We could do the voiceover like this." In a breathy whispery voice, he said, "Here … we find the Bottopotamus … in his natural habitat … on the planet of Bombing Flex."

"This could be just the thing to give the show the ratings boost it needs," Hang added.

"You also need to free all the players from previous shows," said Mitzy.

"What?" said Hang. "But the little Snifflers love meeting all the aliens down at the zoo."

"They're prisoners," said Mitzy.

"But we like them."

"Then don't steal them and lock them up. Invite them to come here."

"Invite them?" said Sloop.

"Yes, as tourists – not zoo animals! All you need to do is get word out about how beautiful your planet is and I bet you'll get loads of aliens visiting. You can even provide the transportation. Although you might want to change the name of the planet."

"What's wrong with Planet Bogey?" asked Sloop, loudly blowing his nose.

"Er…" Mitzy glanced at Biskit. "It doesn't matter. Now, you can start by sending us back to Earth."

"Sending you back?" said Hang. "But you said our planet was beautiful."

"It is," said Biskit, "but you can hardly film *The Biskit Show* without your lead character and his sidekick—"

"Ahem," Mitzy coughed.

"Partner, then," said Biskit.

"We need to go back because our job is to protect those who protect us," said Mitzy.

"Fine. We'll send you back. But tell me this," said Hang. "Why do you feel the need to protect those humans?"

"Because they never ask us to," said Biskit. "They never ask anything of us at all."

"That's right," said Mitzy. "They love us for who we are. This is how we repay them."

The Snatchers sneezed, showering Biskit and Mitzy with Cosmic Snot that sent them flying back through space. Once again, Mitzy felt as helpless as a speck of dust caught in the middle of a hurricane. She felt dizzy and strangely weightless as she watched the shapes and patterns appear in the colours around her.

She landed with a **FLUDUMP!** as solid ground appeared beneath her paws. As the snot dripped away from her eyes, she saw that she and Biskit were standing by the potting shed in the allotments on the hill.

"We're back," barked Biskit. He was about to shake himself dry when he caught Mitzy's eye. "We're home." He rolled over on the ground to dry his fur instead.

"Yes. Back home," repeated Mitzy softly. All her life, her home had been with Cynthia, but that had changed now. At some point she would tell Biskit what had happened in the Players' Palace but now was not the time.

Dark clouds shifted across the black night sky with comforting familiarity. Mitzy looked up and spotted a distant star.

"I'm sorry we never found Champ," she said.

"We learned that Champ is out there somewhere," said Biskit. "That's a start."

"It's a big universe," said Mitzy.

"I won't give up on him," replied Biskit. "Hey, do you think those Snot Snatchers really will film us?"

"Hopefully not," said Mitzy, although she did like the idea that Cynthia could be up on Planet Bogey, watching over her.

"I'm not sure what Commander F will think of it," said Biskit. "We are supposed to be a secret organization after all."

"Yes, good point," said Mitzy. "Maybe we should take him something to eat to soften the news. What do you reckon? A couple of carrots?"

"Good idea. I can smell some up this way." Biskit followed his nose. "Hey, I still can't believe your biggest fear was the Dung Guzzler. I mean, you must have fought other scary things."

"My biggest fear wasn't about me," said Mitzy.

"What does that mean?" Biskit stopped and turned round to face her. The headlight of a passing car lit up her green eyes.

"That time we fought the Dung Guzzler, the first time we met, it electrocuted you. You were unconscious for ages. I thought…" Mitzy looked away then met Biskit's gaze. "I thought I'd lost you."

A slow grin spread across Biskit's face. "So you're saying your biggest fear is losing me?"

Mitzy blushed under her fur then said, "Oh no. My biggest fear is having to ever eat a mushroom again. They were SO revolting."

Biskit laughed.

"I know," he said. "I saw them on the way out. I can never un-see that." He shivered at the memory. "Come on."

The Pet Defenders ventured through the allotments in search of food for their grumpy boss. Neither of them noticed a small green light

from one of the trees as a camera-bot filmed their every move, beaming the pictures across space to Planet Bogey.